Very Busy Barbie

By Barbara Slate

Illustrated by Winslow Mortimer

A GOLDEN BOOK • NEW YORK

Golden Books Publishing Company, Inc., Racine, Wisconsin 53404

On a Tuesday morning Barbie was busy in her kitchen when the telephone rang. "Hello," said Barbie.

"I have great news for you!" said the voice on the other end. "This is Richard, from Lily Fashions. You are one of two finalists in the Lily spokesmodel contest. Can you come to a meeting Thursday at two o'clock in Ms. Lily's office?" Richard continued. "Ms. Lily herself will decide which model will represent her company."

"I wouldn't miss such an exciting opportunity!" answered Barbie.

That afternoon Richard called Laureen, another model. He told her that she, too, was a finalist in the Lily spokesmodel contest.

"Who is the other model?" Laureen asked.

When Richard told her that it was Barbie, Laureen was upset.

"I'm not going to let Barbie win," Laureen said to herself. "I lost the swimsuit cover for *What's In* magazine to her two months ago, but I'll be the Lily spokesmodel if it's the last thing I do!"

The next morning Barbie had to do some volunteer work. Every day she took breakfast to Mrs. Appleberry, an elderly lady in the neighborhood who needed help.

"Good morning," said Barbie when she arrived at Mrs. Appleberry's house.

"Barbie, you're a dear," said Mrs. Appleberry. "You are so good to come every morning."

"It's my pleasure," said Barbie.

Barbie told her friend all about the phone call she had received the day before.

"Oh, Barbie!" cried Mrs. Appleberry. "I hope you win. I know you'd make a wonderful spokesmodel for Lily."

On Thursday morning when Barbie rang the doorbell to Mrs. Appleberry's house, she was surprised that there was no answer.

"I wonder where Mrs. Appleberry could be," thought Barbie. "She knows I'm coming."

When she looked in a window, Barbie was shocked
to see that Mrs. Appleberry had fallen out of her
wheelchair.

Barbie went to a phone on the corner and dialed
911 for an ambulance. Soon the ambulance arrived.
The medics decided to take Mrs. Appleberry to the
hospital. Barbie was right by her side.

When the doctor would allow it, Barbie went in to visit Mrs. Appleberry. "How are you feeling?" asked Barbie.

"Thanks to you, I'm doing all right," said Mrs. Appleberry. "I had a bad fall. My wrist is broken, but the rest of me is still in one piece!

"Oh, my goodness, Barbie!" exclaimed Mrs. Appleberry when a nurse brought her a late lunch. "It's almost two o'clock! Isn't this the day for your meeting with Lily Fashions? If you don't hurry, you'll be late!"

"Don't worry," said Barbie. "Being with you was more important. Anyway, if I hurry, I should be able to make the meeting."

Barbie hailed a taxi outside the hospital. But no sooner had they started down the road than the taxi got a flat tire.

"Sorry, lady," said the driver. "I hope you're not in a hurry. I have to fix this flat."

"Oh, I *am* in a hurry!" said Barbie. "And I only have ten minutes to get to a meeting!"

Just then Barbie saw a bus waiting at the corner.

Barbie ran for the bus and made it just in time.
"Phew!" she said to herself as she sat down. "I hope
nothing else goes wrong today!"

As the bus turned a corner, Barbie couldn't believe her eyes.

"A parade!" she gasped. "I'd better get off this bus and run, or I'll miss the meeting completely!"

Meanwhile Laureen had arrived at Ms. Lily's office.
She was busy convincing Ms. Lily that she would make
the perfect spokesmodel.

"And I would never be late for such an important
meeting," Laureen assured Ms. Lily.

"Well, Laureen, you certainly are beautiful," Ms. Lily
responded. "But I'm looking for other qualities as well.
That's why I wanted to talk to both you and Barbie.
Well, it seems that Barbie isn't coming. In that case—"

Just then Richard, Ms. Lily's assistant, poked his
head into the room.

"Sorry to disturb you, Ms. Lily, but there's a woman
on the phone who insists on talking to you," he
reported.

"Okay, Richard," replied Ms. Lily, "I'll talk to her."

Ms. Lily picked up the phone.

"Hello, my name is Mrs. Appleberry," said the voice on the other end.

Mrs. Appleberry quickly told Ms. Lily all about how Barbie had rescued her and taken her to the hospital that morning. She reassured Ms. Lily that if Barbie wasn't at the meeting yet, she would be there soon.

A few minutes later Barbie arrived.
"I'm so sorry I'm late," she said.
"There's no need to apologize," Ms. Lily replied.
"Your friend Mrs. Appleberry called and told me how
you rescued her—and how you take breakfast to her
every morning."

Ms. Lily held out her hand. "Well, I've made my decision. Congratulations, Barbie," she said. "I'd like you to be the new spokesmodel for Lily Fashions."

"Thank you!" answered a surprised Barbie. "I will be happy to represent your company."

Laureen shook her head. "Not again!" she thought. "First Barbie wins the swimsuit cover, and now this! What has she got that I don't have?"

"Not only are you beautiful, Barbie, but you're a caring person," complimented Ms. Lily. "You're just the kind of spokesmodel I want for Lily."

Barbie turned to Laureen. "I'm sorry, Laureen," she said.

Laureen was still thinking about what Ms. Lily had said. Maybe there was more to modeling than just beauty.

"That's okay, Barbie," said Laureen. Then she smiled a genuine smile. "Congratulations—but don't count me out next time!"